Gustav Klimt was born in Austria in 1862.
To find out who he was, come meet his cat.

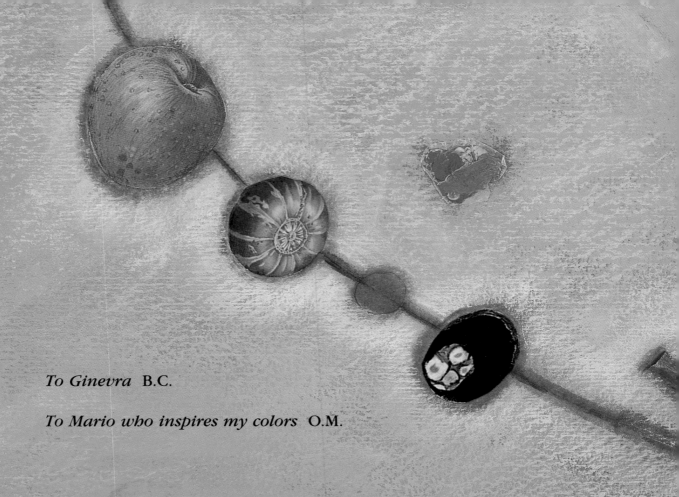

To Ginevra B.C.

To Mario who inspires my colors O.M.

© Edizioni Arka, Milan, Italy 2004

This edition published 2005 in the United States of America by
Eerdmans Books for Young Readers
An imprint of Wm. B. Eerdmans Publishing Company
255 Jefferson SE, Grand Rapids, Michigan 49503
P.O. Box 163, Cambridge CB3 9PU U.K.
www.eerdmans.com

ISBN 0-8028-5282-3

05 06 07 08 09   6 5 4 3 2 1

Printed in Italy

Library of Congress Cataloging-in-Publication Data

Capatti, Berenice.
  Klimt and his cat / written by Berenice Capatti; illustrated by Octavia Monaco.
     p. cm.
  Summary: The life and work of the famous Viennese painter Gustav Klimt is explored by his
favorite cat.
  ISBN 0-8028-5282-3 (alk. paper)
  1. Klimt, Gustav, 1862-1918–Juvenile fiction. [1. Klimt, Gustav, 1862-1918–Fiction. 2. Artists–
Fiction. 3. Painting–Fiction. 4. Cats–Fiction.] I. Monaco, Octavia, ill. II. Title.
  PZ7.C17362Kl 2005
  [E]–dc22
                                                    2004009870

English translation adapted by Shannon A. White

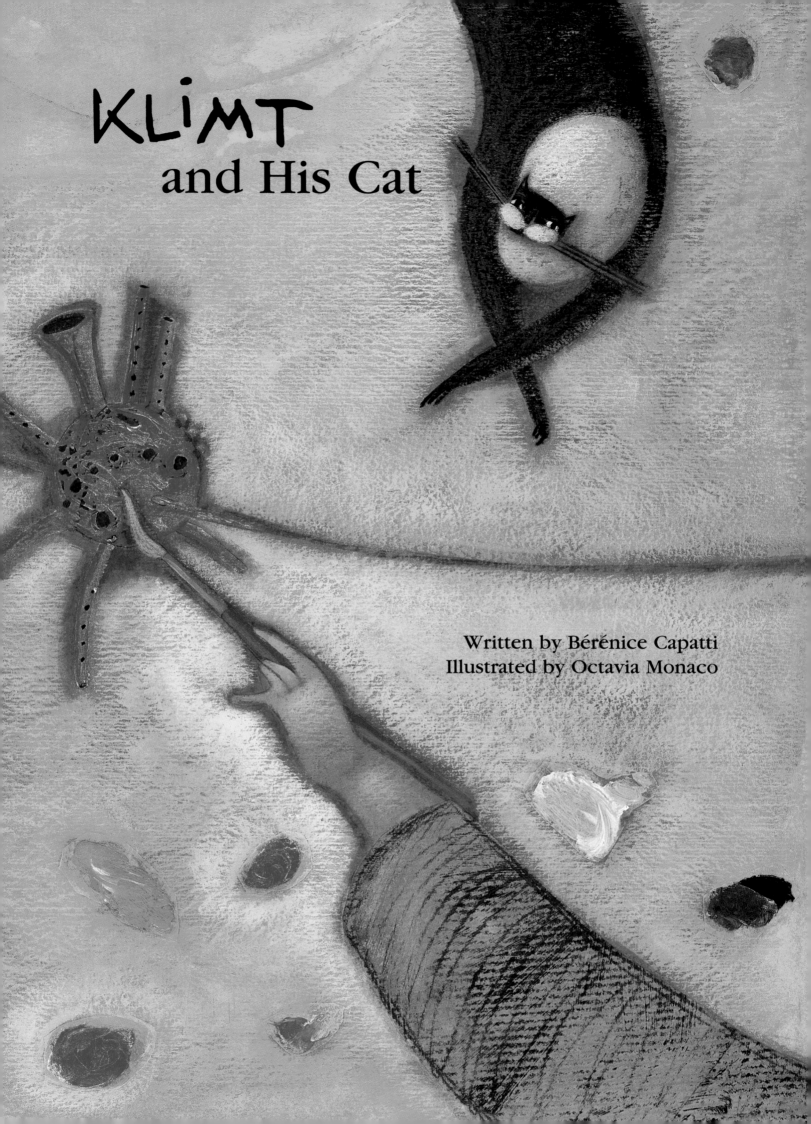

KLIMT
and His Cat

Written by Bérénice Capatti
Illustrated by Octavia Monaco

Follow me into Gustav's studio—it is alive with color! Look at the paintbrushes he keeps in a vase and the reds and blues and colorful hues that spill onto the table. Smell the scent of paint, of oil, of canvas.

You can watch Gustav paint, but he won't know you're there. I often watch him for hours. I mew loudly, I rub against his leg, and I scratch at the chairs but he doesn't see me. He doesn't even hear me. He is absorbed in a world of color and canvas.

Today Gustav is painting a couple in love. Over the figures, he brushes in flowers of gold, the richest of colors.

Roses and flowers of all kinds are painted into his pictures. Gustav is inspired by the garden that blooms outside his window. Early each morning he takes me outside, and together we watch the buds open.

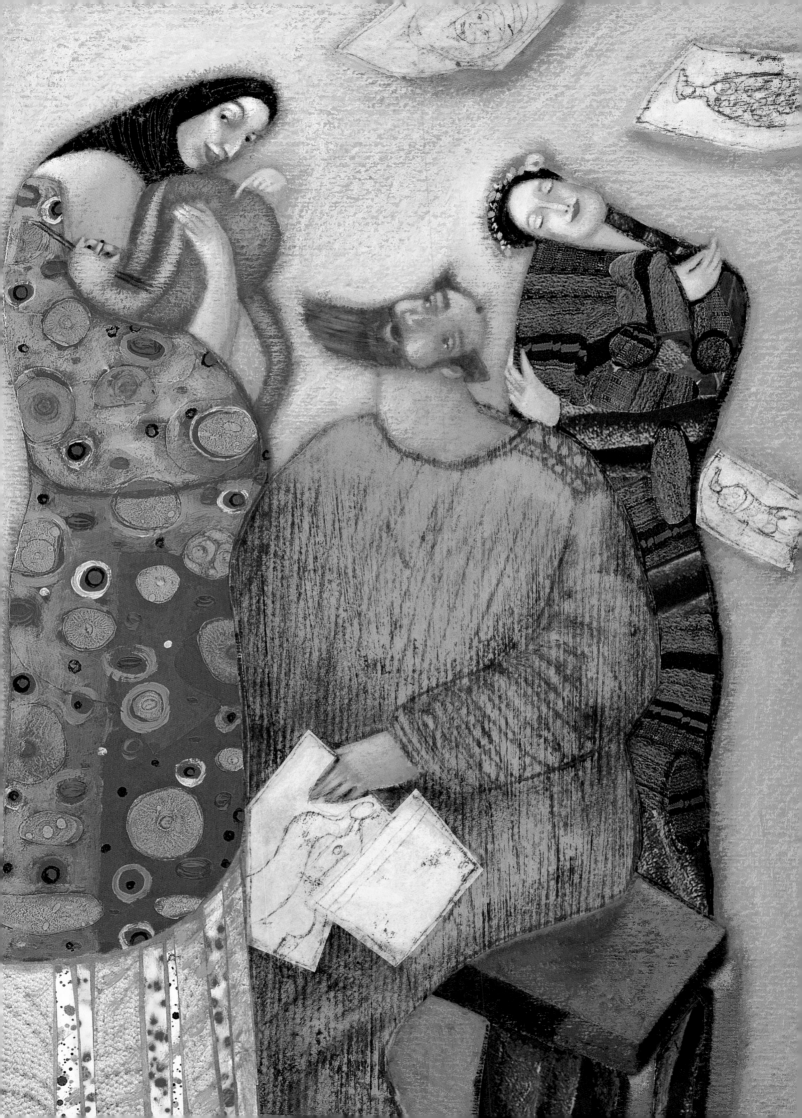

Gustav loves to paint people, so he invites models to his studio to pose for him. I snuggle up against their legs and vie for attention, but Gustav has instructed the models to stay very still while he paints them.

As you can see, when models come, Gustav is messy! Look at all the sketches he throws about the room.

"Katze," he says, catching me staring at the clutter, "painting people requires a great deal of practice!"

It seems to me that it also requires a lot of paper!

I often follow along at the museum while Gustav studies ancient art from Syria, Greece, Egypt, and even China. Gustav says that looking at the paintings and sculptures of other artists helps him as an artist.

"To learn to do better, I must see everything!" he exclaims. "Even works of art that aren't so beautiful."

Walking around the museum with a small red sketchbook, he pencils in notes and makes small drawings of the things he likes—the smile of a beautiful woman, the gentle arch of a doorway. Back at the studio he will use these sketches to decorate the edges of his paintings and make them special.

With splotches of swirls and shapes and golden and silver paint, Gustav creates a new style of art, different from the traditional paintings of the past. Other artists, friends of Gustav's—painters, architects, and sculptors—have helped him construct a building where his art and other new styles of art can be displayed. These artists have called themselves "Secessionists" because they do not want to make traditional art; they do not like to see the same thing over and over again.

Not everyone appreciates the new styles of Gustav and his friends, however. While I am admiring Gustav's new building, a man next to me points at the roof and grumbles: "Katze, what kind of roof is that, a golden cauliflower?" I don't reply; I am pretending that the cauliflower is on his head!

Gustav has taught me that it takes courage to try something new. When he was asked to paint three large works for the University of Vienna, he painted what he felt. Using vibrant color and shapes of all sizes, he portrayed love and life, and sadness too. The University professors, expecting traditional art, are angered at Gustav's work.

Their criticism is so harsh that Gustav buys his paintings back from them.

"Katze, what's important to me is not how many people like my art, but who appreciates it," he says to me, winking. Perhaps he is asking if I like it?

Today we are off to Italy, where we will discover new artists and see wonderful sights! I wander the streets of Venice to look for other cats, but Gustav is interested only in art. He keeps me in his sight as we enter an ancient church.

There before us a magnificent mosaic made up of thousands of glimmering colored glass fragments shines. Even I stop to admire it, totally enchanted, though I understand next to nothing about art. Gustav contemplates it for hours, dreaming of how to use the design in a masterpiece.

Though he enjoys short trips to sightsee, Gustav's real travels take place inside his studio. He is transported to distant lands as he sweeps paint onto paper and details intricate patterns of circles and squares.

Today he paints Emilie, his closest friend. I don't mind that they sometimes walk out into the garden alone because now there are seven more cats in the house—plenty of friends for me!

Emilie and her sisters, who own the most famous dressmaker's boutique in Vienna, often model for Gustav. They wear elaborate fashionable dresses from London, and they are always changing their clothes. Gustav meticulously paints every detail of their dresses, but he doesn't pay much attention to his own attire—every day he wears the same worn-out smock!

Today we are going on vacation! Together with Emilie and her family, we head for the shores of Lake Attersee.

Though we are supposed to be taking a break from our normal routine, Gustav cannot stop being an artist. Even here he works. His favorite spot to paint is in the middle of the lake, where he is fascinated by the reflections. He sees curves of beautiful women swimming in the waves, but all I can see is bright blue water.

Back home Gustav paints people and patterns, but on holiday he paints nothing but landscapes. Maybe he is taking a vacation after all.

When we return to Vienna, Gustav hurries back to the studio, ready to create new compositions. He has much energy to paint these days. He says he feels called to battle the sickness, greed, and unhappiness in the world through his paintings. Gustav knows that art, poetry, and music have the power to make people happy.

I imagine him as an armed soldier, fighting for happiness, leading an army of Viennese citizens right into one of his vibrant paintings, perhaps into the mural he painted in honor of the great musician Beethoven.

Gustav soon returns to painting figures. I try to play with the fancy rich women who are modeling in extravagant clothes, but Gustav reminds me that they must keep still.
Living with a great artist is not always easy!

One afternoon I peek over Gustav's shoulder as he sketches. I watch as the forms of a man and a woman emerge, clutched in an embrace. I already know this is going to be a masterpiece. Gustav crafts the most elaborate and delicate garments in this painting and layers on many ounces of gold, as if to say, "Love is all the wealth you need."

As I look more closely at the finished work, I realize that Gustav was inspired by the design of the shiny glass shapes of the mural we saw in Italy.

Gustav is loyal and generous. Last year, he learned that a local shop was going bankrupt, so he decided to help the owner by purchasing all of his art supplies there.

This afternoon he is lost in thought and does not hear the voice of the beggar in the street. I nudge him gently, and he rushes outside to give the poor man a coin. He always gives money to the needy. Even when he does not want to be disturbed, he leaves a bowl of coins outside his door for them. I think it's a bit strange that the more gold Gustav puts in his paintings, the less he keeps for himself!

Mostly Gustav is full of life. I often hear him laugh, and I love to watch the vigor of his hands swirling colors together, but he is quiet at the moment.

"Katze," he says while scratching my neck, "I am afraid that the young students no longer like my style of art." He looks off in the distance. "I don't even know if they remember me."

Under his gentle touch, I purr loudly, reminding him that he will not be forgotten.

When I look up at the easel after my nap, I am surprised to see that Gustav has created a painting in a completely different style. Soft lines and gentle colors have replaced the decorative circles and squares and gold paint.

Judith

Cradle

Love

Portrait of Adele Bloch Bauer

Portrait of Emilie Floge

"I don't have the gift of the spoken or the written word, Katze," Gustav says to me later that day. "Especially if I have to say something about myself or my work. But whoever wants to know something about me as an artist," he continues, gesturing at his paintings that lie scattered about the studio, "ought to look carefully at my pictures and try to see in them what I am and what I want to do."

As usual, I don't reply. I simply breathe in deeply and inhale the scents of oil, of paint, and of canvas.

Gustav Klimt died in 1918. Here are some of his paintings.

Yearning for Happiness,
detail of *Beethoven Frieze*

The Cavalier, detail of
Beethoven Frieze

*The Three Ages
of Woman*

Music

Medicine

The Kiss